Mystery of the Lake

By Teresa Comeau

This is dedicated to my parents Paul and Modeste,

As well as my friend Michelle

Thanks to you all!!!!

^ ^ ^

It's summer. It has been few nightmarish years since the accidents, as my mother calls them. Have you ever noticed how swiftly people's lives can change? I mean, one minute you can be happy as a child, the next angry as a mule. You know, it's the time after that.

I'm going to tell you a story, my story. The first few years I had to go to the hospital. It was for therapy. In telling you this I can't leave out anything. No I can't.

I was sixteen, at the time. Jack and Annie were seventeen. Jack disappeared right after and I haven't seen him since. It's hard for me to tell this story, especially about Jack. I was in love with him.

* * *

Bang! "What was that?" I asked myself, in a low voice. I got up from bed and put my pillow, in its place. The book I was reading balanced on the edge of the bed.

When I got down stairs, I found my sister, at the table. Mom was cleaning the mess, she had made with the blender. "What happened?" I asked holding the blending up for her. "I went outside, to feed the cat and Sandie put a carrot and an egg in the blender," she stated," you see what happened with no lid." Mom was so made and yelled at Sandie again. "Really you almost eleven you should know better!"

I stuck my head out the door and let the warm summer sun shine on my face, it felt so warm. The phone rang and mom answered it. "Who is it?" I asked. "It was your father. He's at the airport," she said with a big smile, "Jack and Annie are there. He's driving them over right away." "Yes, Yes, Yes!!!" I said excited running upstairs to get ready for their arrival.

I cleaned my room, had a shower and did my hair. Then I heard the car door. I looked out the window and there they were Jack and

Annie, my two best friends. I hurried downstairs and out the front door. Excitedly I gave them each a big hug and kiss. We all went inside and put there things in there new rooms.

That afternoon, my parents drove my sister Sandie to her friend's house. Then they went to the airport and left with Mr. and Mrs. Smith. The Smiths are Jack and Annie parents. There okay, I guess but not as cool as my parents.

Jack and Annie are twins. They have brown hair and eyes. Jack's fifteen minutes older. He's muscled and thinks he was twenty-five, instead of seventeen. Jack's into weights, muscle cars and motorcycles. His hair is short but very stylish, kind of hot, like you just want to run your fingers through it. What he loves to do most is drive his bike.

Annie, on the other hand, is petite and very stylish. She's more into politics and save the planet campaigns. She has long hair and it's always done up in a braid or something neat. There's never a strand of hair out of place.

Then there's me, my name is Alexandra but my friends call me Alex. That is everyone except Jack; he calls me by full name and never said why. I'm sixteen. I'm the chubby girl of the family but I try to stay well dressed. In the summer usually dressy shorts, I love silk. I think Jack likes them. There's another thing you must know about me, I love Jack but he doesn't know.

* * *

Ring-g-g-g! It was the phone. So I answered it I my room. "Hello, you reached the Parker residence. This is Alex, may I help you?" I laughed to myself. Mom and dad are business people and sometimes there clients call. I think it's stupid and laugh every time I say it. "Hi Alex this is Antony. How are you?" "I'm fine. What's up?" Antony said, "I wanted to know if you wanted to go swimming? Laura said it was ok." Laura is the owner of the lake near our house. She's very nice and always says yes, when we want to go swimming. I think it's because she couldn't have kids and feel we're hers in a way. "Antony, I can't. I have company for the summer, maybe later in the afternoon, okay." I said. "Yeah sure," she sounded pissed and hung up. So I just put the receiver on the hook. I told the others it was Antony and we continued with our conversation.

We went downstairs after a while and I asked them if they wanted anything to drink. Jack of course wanted a beer and Annie a cup of tea. I had a glass wine. My parents were pretty lenient about underage drinking. Their philosophy was as long as we act responsibly, they wouldn't take the alcohol away. So we always drank carefully and made sure no other adults seen us. We sat down at the kitchen table and kept talking until four o'clock. Then I asked them about going to the lake to see Antony. We all agree and went.

When we got there we were shocked to find Antony frozen, in the lake. Annie and I screamed and put our heads in Jack's shoulder. I looked up and saw a doll. The doll was bright red and near Laura's place.

I left Annie, on Jack's shoulder and went to the doll. Picking the doll up, I saw it turn a brighter red. Jack yelled, "What's that?" I walked back to him and showed him the doll. "It looks like the devil," I said. I gave it to Annie so she could study it further. She had studied demonology early in high school. She might know what it is, but she didn't. Jack didn't know either. So she put in her jacket and we went home.

We walked into the house and smelled something burning. It was Annie's jacket pocket. It fell to the floor….. Annie picked it up, ran upstairs and hid it. After that I phoned Laura and then the police. They arrived at my house twenty minutes later. I told them everything that I knew, well not everything. I left the doll out. They talked to me for about half hour and then they interrogated Jack and Annie it seemed forever but actually it was only for a half hour also.

When they left we sat down and had a few drinks even Annie did, w3hich is weird but this was a strange day. I never had anyone close to me die. Antony was my age. 16! No one so young should die, especially frozen in a lake in the summer.

* * *

Two days later, after everything including us had calmed down, we went looking for clues. I suggested we go looking around Laura's place because that's where the doll was. Jack thought it was stupid but agreed and so did Annie. We looked but didn't find anything. We looked around Laura', the lake, in the ditches and couldn't find nothing. That was pretty fringing weird. People leave clues. People forget things. What's going on????

I decided to take a walk toward the landing where Antony's body was frozen and began to cry. I never cry... I was thinking that it could have been us, if we would have gone swimming earlier and I cried even more. Who would have thought that a summer with my best friends could have turned this way? First a murder with a mystery attached.

Jack and Annie still looking for clues didn't notice me, until I was kneeling on the ground, with my hands on my face. Jack ran to me and took me into his arms. Annie looked at me with tears in her eyes. Jack then picked me up and carried me home. Annie was in front with the keys to the house.

I was still crying when Jack carried me to my room. "Alexandra," he said, "are you going to be all right?" "Jack, I'll be fine. I want to sleep for a while," I said in a low shaky voice. I closed my eyes and fell asleep. Jack and Annie were talking when they left. The door closed and everything was silent.

"Alexandra, I ……" Silence "Anyway I'll be here whenever you need me," he said. Then he bent and kissed my forehead. I don't remember if he left because I fell asleep.

* * *

Two other kids were found frozen in the lake. It was then quarantined off and Laura was put under surveillance and we were drawn to the mystery. With all the places, we found one clue so far. So what did the doll and Laura have in common? I've known Laura all my life; she can't have anything to do with this.

I had a dream that night. I felt something pulling towards the lake. It was a strong and strange feeling. Annie saw me and yelled for Jack. I was sleepwalking; I have never sleepwalked in my life until that night. I was walking toward the lake and had one foot in the water when Jack pulled me away. When I woke up, I was on the lawn. They looked at me in horror. So I looked down and saw what they saw. "My foot," I screamed. It was red, blistery and swollen, I fainted.

- -

Waking up in the doctor's office, I looked around. Then I spotted the doctor and felt a cold shiver sweep over me. It felt as if he was connected to the doll but that was nonsense. He looked at my foot gave me some cream and said it would be better in a day or two. It just looked worse then what it actually was.

....

When we got home, I told Annie and Jack what I had felt. They started to laugh but I told them again. That time I guess I was a little more pissed because they began to believe me.

.....

I slept uneasily that night. I kept thinking about what had happened.

* * *

Today is the 20th of July. It's a nice day where nothing can go wrong. At least nothing should have. So we decided to have a picnic among the tree. We packed up everything we needed and started walking. When we arrived Annie happily chose a spot in a shaded area.

We set up the blanket and held it down it rocks. As we set out the meats and cheese, Annie saw four bottles of beer. They were hidden at the bottom of the basket. "What's this? Jack!" Annie shouted. I began to laugh, while Jack just sat back grinning like a fox. Annie sat there and started to think about it some more and started to laugh about it herself.

"I'm sorry," Annie apologized to Jack, "I shouldn't have overreacted. I mean, we only get one life to live. So, what's the sense of acting so uptight about everything?" "You're right, you should have more fun," he flashed his handsome smile, "shouldn't she, Alexandra?" I returned the smile and said, "Yeah." Then turned away and blushed a bright red.

As we ate and drank we told stories. I had told Annie a secret the month before; know she was going to tease me. "Oh Jack!" she said, "I know a secret you should hear." He looked at her curiously, "what is it?" I drank my beer and listened. "Alex told me, that she had a dream about the two of you!" I grabbed her by the arm and said very pissed off, "Tell and die!!" Then she stopped and looked at me shocked. Turned around and burst out laughing. It was too late though Jack wanted to know, now. Annie kept saying NO but Jack will find out, he always does when he has his mind set on something but he stopped for now.

We were all done eating and we had food left. I felt a little bit mischievous so I started a food fight. OMG, it was so much fun. Laura heard all the noise and came running out way thinking we were in trouble. Shit!!!!! She started yelling at us. This is totally out of character. She's usually so sweet. "You kids leave before I call the cops." She yelled. "Alex, I have your parents' number; behave or I'll call them and they'll be home before you know it." I apologized.

I went to Laura and gave her a hug and said that we'd never do it again and that if she needed anything to give us a call. I also asked if she had any idea what was going on and she said no and started to cry and went home. We all felt bad because the cops will not leave her alone.

* * *

We walked home and something shinned in the bushes. I went over and picked it up. Jack and Annie wanted to see what I was holding. "What is it?" They said in unison. "It's some kind of gold plate," I stated. Jack took it from my hands and dusted it off. "Look at this." He lifted it up and had a name on it. "Let me see," Annie said quickly. She turned it over and over. Then she told us the name that was inscribed on it.

It was VANDERMEER

"I studied various European languages but I don't know what it means," Annie said, "Let's go back to the house, I have to check some books." So we went back to the house. When we arrived, Annie took the metal plate upstairs. Jack and I waited downstairs.

"What's going on?" I asked Annie desperately. "I don't know, I just don't know anymore," Jack said. "Alexandra, do you think we'll die to?" I told him not to worry and that everything would be fine. I was worried to but didn't want to tell him. We went and grabbed a few bottles of beer for him and a bottle of wine for me and went into the living room to watch TV; while we wait for Annie.

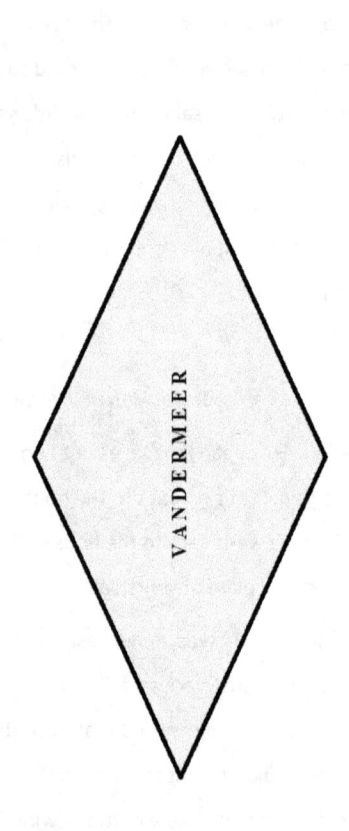

It was the news; they announced that six other kids had disappeared. Oh shit!!!! "When will it end?" he asked me. "I don't know, Jack, I really don't." So we turned the channel and watched a comedy that was on. Anything is better than the news and real life.

Annie came down finally after four hours. She said that she couldn't find anything. We knew it wasn't true, but we let it be. After that it we had supper. We weren't very hungry but we ate anyway. We separated after and it seemed that we just wanted to be alone. We all wanted to do work. Like our own little research. I kept thinking, why was I drawn to the lake and you could tell Jack was worried about Annie and Annie was hiding something.

I had a funny feeling and went and knocked on Jack's door. He said to come in. He was lying on the bed starring at the ceiling and looked very sad. "What's wrong?" I asked but he would answer. "Jack, didn't you find Annie acting suspicious?" He still didn't say anything. I say the look on his face. After a few minutes he said, "She usually comes and talk to me when something's up." I think he said it more to himself then to me. He then turned to me and said, "Something is wrong and she doesn't want me, NO us to worry."

"Jack, I know. I've had that feeling. I'll leave, just in case she comes," I gave him a hug and left.

I listened to music hoping that Annie or Jack would come and talk. Nothing! So I laid there thinking about the murders. I noticed that it was only kids. But after the first two the lake was quarantined off and there is no way anyone that I know would go near the place. If you look on Facebook or twitter it's all the news and how everyone's scared. Look what happened to me though, I was asleep and I got hurt. Could it be that they others died while sleepwalking. Hum!!!

I used to be so close to Annie and with everything happening it's like I need Jack more. It's like he's the only one that can protect me. She's been acting differently for a while, I thought it was cause she found a boyfriend but she hasn't called anyone. It's strange!

* * *

Today is Tuesday, I woke up at 6 am and went outside and checked the newspaper. As I was reading through it, I saw the article about mysterious deaths. Then I ran to wake up Jack and Annie. When we were, in the kitchen having tea and milk, I showed them the article. Annie took it and ran upstairs.

"There's something wrong with Annie," I told Jack. "I know!" Jack said worried. After a while we went to see Annie and she finally told us what she had discovered. What VANDERMEER had meant; dweller at or near a lake.

Later that day Joan called. She asked if I had seen Leana and I said no. After I hung up, I ran to the lake, Annie and Jack behind me. Then and there I saw her, my cousins' figure, in the lake and I started to cry. Again Jack and Annie took me home and put me to bed. Later when I was sleeping uneasily, I heard someone come into my room and kiss me on the cheek. I knew it was Jack.

When I woke, I called my aunt Joan and told her what had happened. She started to cry and hung up. After that I didn't hear from her again. So I went to the kitchen and made myself a peanut butter and jam sandwich.

As I was waiting for Jack and Annie, I thought about Leana. When they entered I had tears in my eyes. "Annie, Jack can I fix you anything to eat?" I asked wiping the tears away. "No," they answered together. After I was done, we went into the living room and watched TV.

Sitting here, I kept thinking of everything that has happened. I looked at Jack and then to Annie, they never even realized. There zoned into the TV. I kept thinking of what Annie had said about the gold plate. The only thing dwelling near the lake is Laura and a bunch of trees. Could Laura have something to do with it? She has treated us like family but lately there has been some strange going on there. Naw, not Laura…….

* * *

It was a cloudy day and I was taking a walk with Jack. It was a week after my cousin Leana death. Jack and I were holding hands, it made me feel safe and his skin felt so good. As I said before Jack and I got closer and this was nice. We were walking down the path near the lake, when all of a sudden, it started to rain. I told Jack that there was a cabin up the path. I was only wearing a t-shirt and a pair of shorts. Jack was wearing a t-shirt, jeans his leather jacket and boots of course. I don't know why he wears that year round because it gets so hot, it mustn't be cool.

The rain rolled down, on his face. It was so nerving, that it drove me with wild desire for Jack right know. Then I heard his voice telling me to run for the cabin. Even when I came back from trance, he still was a hot piece of meat.

As we reached the cabin, I screamed. He asked me why. I pointed to it. He assured me that it was a harmless grass snake looking for shelter. Then turning we went inside. It was dark, so Jack lit a match to look around. There was a candle on the mantle, so he lit it, after he made a fire, in the fireplace and we relaxed, on the floor.

Nonchalantly he put his arm around my shoulders and whispered in my ear sweetly, "I love you!" We kissed. He told me, he loved my hair in the sunshine and my eyes when I get curious. I was tired and still cold. Jack told me to lie down beside him and gave me three more quick kisses. The first was on the forehead, second on the check and the third on the lips. As I fell asleep I could feel Jack warmth slide over me and I snuggled even closer.

I woke up about half hour later and Jack was staring at me. I sat up and he grabbed me and gave me a long passionate kiss. There was a strange noise at the door. Jack went to see, nothing! So he started kissing me again. He stopped for a few minutes and went and grabbed an old blanket that was in the other room of the cabin and laid it on the floor. Jack then slowly laid me to the blanket and started to kiss me from the top of my head to the tip of my toes. I felt so how and responded to his every touch. Taking his lead, I slowly removed his t-shirt and kissed his warm chest.

OMG, I can't believe this is happening. He feels so warm and silky. I never knew he had tattoos. We slowly explored each other. The Jack said, "Alexandra I don't want to hurt you." I replied, "You never could!" He then slowly took me and I bit into his shoulder. I felt so much joy as I let out a little yelp. Jack made sure I was satisfied and then he came with a strong force.

We laid there and snuggle for a few minutes and caught our breaths. Eventually, when we realized it had stopped raining we got dressed, gave each other a few quick kisses and left for the house.

I wore his jacket home and it felt really good. We never talked about what happened at the cabin when we got home and Annie never suspected anything. While talking to Annie in the kitchen, at the table, Jack took my hand and squeezed it. Nothing was said again about the cabin and what happened.

* * *

Annie on the other hand noticed the length that we were gone and was going tease us all night long. "Well, well you two were gone a long time," she said with a smirk. "For your info we had to stop at a cabin because of the rain," I told her. Then I started laughing but was interrupted by Jack. "True and what did you make for supper Annie?" Jack said a little pissed off. "Nothing because I didn't know when you'd be back!" she said harshly. "What the fuck do you think we're going to eat!" he said very angrily. Jack was almost ready to hit her, when I interrupted, "relax, I'll fix you something."

"That was mighty fine grub, Alexandra" he said as if nothing had happened earlier. "Well Jack your very nice to Alex," Annie said, "what got into you today?" He snapped back to her, "I just wanted to see what you'd say!" I just sat back and laughed at them. They always fought like cats and dogs. Thank god Sandie and I don't do that much.

After that episode we went our separate ways for the evening. I listened to music. Annie was still trying to figure out what's happening with the doll. Jack the jerk went on a date with Nadine. He goes out with the bimbo like nothing happened. Men can't live with 'em; can't live without 'em.

I watched through the window as Jack came home and he looked at me spying on him. He gave me a quick wink and a smile. It was his way of telling me that it was all for show and so Annie wouldn't suspect anything.

* * *

The next week everything had gone well and nobody had gotten killed. We were all so glad. I didn't speak to Jack unless it was very necessary. Annie was amused, of the silent treatment. Jack on the other hand wasn't. Nobody has ever acted this way towards him, but I want to show him that I'm not like all the other girls. I'm his best friend!!

Finally, Annie couldn't stand it anymore and broke the ice. "Let's go for a picnic." "Why?" I replied. I wasn't really into it, plus it meant to be closer to Jack. "Do we have to?" Jack whined with a smile on his face. "You don't have to come," she replied quickly, "but you are!" So we finally agreed, packed some food and left.

On the way Jack yelled and pointed in a direction. We looked where he was pointing, it was at the lake. There were five more kids frozen, but they were different from the others. The others were in one piece but these weren't. These kids were mutilated except for their heads. They were intact but the rest of the bodies were all over the lake. The water wasn't blue anymore; it was red like the devil himself.

We thought the lake was frozen cause of a freak of nature. We were wrong! The doll Annie had put in her pocket a few weeks ago, started to heat up again. Then it melted the other pocket and fell to the ground. The DOLL, I couldn't believe it, she brought it with her. It started to move. OMG! OMG! OMG!

There was something huge coming out, of the lake. It started to talk. It said its name was Uniak Vandermeer, cousin of the devil. I went and hid behind Jack. I was so frightened but Jack started towards it. I tried to stop him but he pulled away. "Why have you been killing these poor kids, asshole?" He shouted at Vandermeer. Jack was clenching his fists. I have never seen Jack so mad in my life. Uniak Vandermeer said very politely, "Well my dear boy because I've been told too by my cousin." I couldn't believe the cousin, of the devil, could have such manners. Uniak Vandermeer was very well dressed, had great manners but there's one thing about hi I didn't like. He was huge and I couldn't see his eyes. If I can't see someone's eyes, I can't tell if there sincere or not. This is one of those cases.

As we talked I found out more, Annie she was in a trance. I told myself, "Allie get ahold of yourself it's only a dream!!!" Yeah, a dream that explains it but…. Jack went to his sister, pulled her away and then he pulled me away. I think Jack knew what was going on. It was trying to get us into the water. If we were in the water we would be dead and no one could stop him. What he didn't know is that Annie finally figure out what to do when she seen him. So when Jack pulled her away she was finally able to piece everything together. She had whispered it in our ears and we ran home; got a few things.

- - - - - - - - - - - - - -

When we got close to the lake we hid in the wood and got everything ready. Jack had the metal rod in his hands. We crept closer to the lake so Uniak Vandermeer didn't see use. Annie instructed Jack to put the rod in the water and we didn't know why. Jack did it anyway. We are going to do as she says cause she's the one that's been doing the research and knows what she's doing I think. The look in Annie eyes was terrifying and we knew it was our old Annie.

"Alexandra, I'm so scared for her," he said holding back tears, in his voice, "It looks like she's hypnotized but she's not." "I know but….." I couldn't finish my sentence. I went over and gave Jack a hug and went on doing as we were told.

We had put the rod, in the water like she said and we watched. She looped the doll on the doll and let it slide towards the water. Annie looked at us with a big smile on her face. We hoped it was for a good reason. The she yelled, "RUN, it's gonna blow!!!" We ran for cover.

BOOOOOMMMMMMM!!!!!!

We looked at each other with a happy grin. There was ice everywhere. We knew then that everything was going to be fine. Who would have thought that the doll would be the savior?

You saw Vandermeer explode into a dozen pieces.

"What happened?" I asked Annie. "Well," she said, "I just figured that the doll was attached to someone and let's face it, it looked like him. So I took a chance that if both the doll and Vandermeer occupied the same space it would be volatile." I have to admit the doll had looked like him. When it comes to evil who knows what works. The dark arts are a mystery to Jack and I. Annie loves the stuff. I swear if Harry Potter was real she would be right there fighting battles and playing with magic, lol.

The sky turned red as blood. The water started to boil; then appeared the DEVIL. "You've killed my cousin," he said, "prepare to die!" Jack standing there told him to go fuck a cow. Jack also told him if he hurt any of us that he'd kill him with his bare hands. The devil responded with a laugh that cut right through you. "My dear child you can't hurt me but I'm going to hurt you," he said.

The devil was ready to throw fireballs, when we heard a voice. I looked around but couldn't see anyone. "My dear brother if I told you more than once over the centuries, you're never to hurt my children," it said. Astounded by what we heard we looked to the heavens. The clouds started to part and a bright light shown down.

The voice was coming from inside the bright light. It spoke again this time to us. "Jack Smith step into my light," it said. The devil tried to stop Jack but couldn't. Jack had stepped into the light with apprehension and it had started to glow. "Now you have the power to beat my brother if he wishes to continue fighting." It was the last thing the voice said and then the bright light disappeared. We are now alone. Well not really the devil is still here.

Annie and I looked at Jack scared. He was still glowing. Jack said to the devil it's up to you what happens this can end right known and we can walk away. Vandermeer had killed those children and he had to be stopped, nothing has to happen between us but if it does be prepared for the end….. The devil wanted a fight!

Jack put his hands up, rain started; thunder sounded and then there was lightning. The devil threw fireballs and sharp knives at Jack. Every one bounced off of him. We couldn't believe the damage that was happening around them; trees exploding, rock shattering and Laura's house collapse. Then with a final shake, of his hands, Jack threw everything he was given into the lake. There was a big explosion and blood splatter everywhere. The lake evaporated and Jack stopped glowing. He fell to the ground. Annie and I looked up and the devil was gone. Then we looked at the empty lake and from the middle came a fresh spring of blue water, as hope, happiness was in the future.

The sky was turning blue. Everyone was coming out of their houses and started jumping for joy. Annie and I ran to Jack and gave him a hug. We looked at the people hugging each other in relief and joy for a minute. I turned to give Jack another hug and he was gone.

Annie and I looked everywhere for him. We knocked on doors and asked everyone but no one had seen him leave. "Oh My God! What are we going to do?" I asked Annie. "Allie, he's ok," she said, "and don't worry he'll be back. Jack loves you, I know he does." Annie pulled me closer and we walked home.

* * *

Two days later our parents arrived with Sandie. We told Mr. and Mrs. Smith that Jack had disappeared and they called the police. My mom and dad gave me a big hug, even Sandie did. We explained to our parents what happened when they were gone and they were shocked and started to cry. Crying for the dead children but also for what we had gone through.

Annie and her parents stayed while the police looked for Jack. They search for two weeks. The police wanted to pronounce him dead even without a body. We finally convinced them to keep the case open. I mean we know he's alive; it's just that he's trying to deal with things. The Smith's went home. I'm going to miss my best friend. I couldn't deal with none of it and went into shock.

A month had gone by and I was still in shock my dad put me in the hospital. I was not surprised but when they ran the standard test for admittance they found out I was pregnant. My parents were in shock then.

I was settling in well at the hospital, getting fat but was not talking. As long as I was not ready to deal with what happened they

would not let me go home. My doctors' name was Leonard Iolas and he was very nice. He talked to me and encouraged me. Dr. Iolas let me know that it was normal for me to feel this way and even if I wasn't going to cooperate with him and talk; he wouldn't let them take the baby. The doctor told me that the baby would a good part of Jack. I snapped at the doctor then. "Dr. Iolas I'd rather have Jack then the baby!" I said in tears. The doctor was so happy to hear me speak he said, "Allie you're on the way to the healing and I promise it will be better." Seven months later I gave birth to Jack Jr. and as promised I was able to keep the baby with me. -------
----

Jack Jr. and I have been living in the hospital know for the last two years. I've gotten a letters from Annie saying that she's gotten married and pregnant. Wow, Annie is nineteen and married who would have thought. I'm happy for her. She's having a girl and the name she picked is Maria Alexandra. Everyone had recovered from the incident but me. Maybe if I knew what happened to Jack, I could go on. I mean I'm doing good considering and so is J.J...

My sister comes to visit and she's so excited. She finally has a boyfriend. I looked at her with a tear in my eye. Now it's me and

J.J…. I mean I miss everyone, especially Jack he was my best friend. We take people for granted and when there gone we go crazy. I said to myself, "why can't I let him go?"

^^ *** ^^

It was a Wednesday and Dr. Iolas came to see me, "Alexandra, I have a visitor waiting for you! Let me take J.J. and you can visit," he said to me kind of cheerful. "Don't you ever call me that!!?" I said harshly, "only Jack calls me that. But yes take him and I'll visit with my company." The doctor tool Jack Junior with him and a few minutes later I heard the door open behind me. Thinking it was my mom or dad I wasn't in a rush to turn around, until I heard the voice. "Alexandra, I never want to hear you speak to your doctor like that again.' The voice said. I turned around quickly and saw Jack standing there. I fainted.

I woke up a few minutes later and was so happy to see him. "Jack," I said, "is it really you?" "Yes it is and I'm sorry," he said. "Alexandra I had to come back because I love you and I want to be with you forever. Will you be my wife?" I looked at him in awe. "Umm Jack there's something I got to tell you first before I give you and answer," I said. He looked shocked that my answer wasn't yes right away. I went over to the phone and asked the nurse to bring J.J. in to me. A happy little toddler strolls in and gives me a big hug. "Jack, I'd like you to meet J.J., he's you son." I said to him. It was Jack's turn to be shocked. "Ah are you sure? How old is he? Oh my god!" he stammered. I explained to Jack everything and as we talked I introduced J.J to his father. As father and son got to know each other, I looked at them very happy. Looking at Jack, I asked is the question still on the table. He looked at me and shook his head yes. I said to Jack, "Yes I'll marry you."

After a few days and Jack being there constantly the doctor let me go home with him. My parents cried when I told them I was getting married and moving away with Jack. We had to get away. Plus Jack had a good job and an apartment. He had just come back to get me. So before we left; we had a quick wedding. Jack junior had fun, actually we all did and within no time I was pregnant again.

Just to let you know that we have been married for almost fifty years. We have six children and twelve grandchildren. Believe it or not we have two great grandchildren. The other amazing thing is nothing that happened when we were teenagers ever happened again!!

Teresa Comeau was born and raised on the French Shore of Nova Scotia, Canada.

Brought up in a small fishing community, she finished high school & went off to college.

She started studying culinary arts but it was not a passion & went on working in different fields.

Finally she studied continuing care assistant because she loved the work but her true passion was still in writing and performing arts.

She continues to do what she loves and believes everyone should follow their dreams.

www.ingramcontent.com/pod-product-compliance
Lightning Source LLC
Chambersburg PA
CBHW071225130626
46555CB00004B/1847